let's look at

clothes

Nicola Tuxworth

Getting dressed

We usually get dressed in the morning.

stripey socks

cotton dungarees

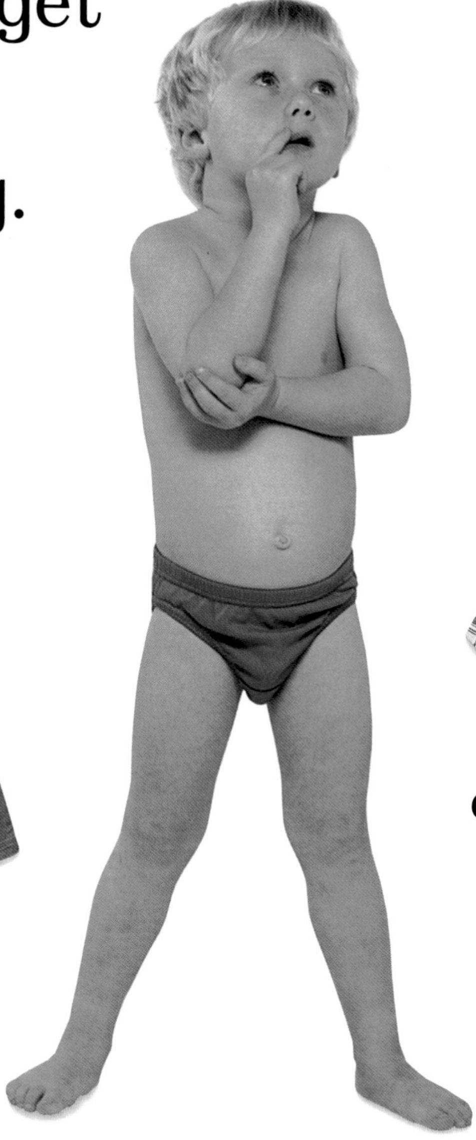

What shall I wear today?

checked shirt

red shoes

First I put
on my socks ...

... then my
shirt ...

. and
hen my
ungarees!

Last of all,
I put on
my shoes.

Tops...

These clothes are for the top half of our bodies ...

knitted cardigan

long-sleeved blouse

sleeveless shirt

comfy sweatshirt

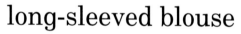

summer jacket

..and bottoms

. and these clothes
re for the bottom
alf of our bodies.

lace-up
pumps

woolly
socks

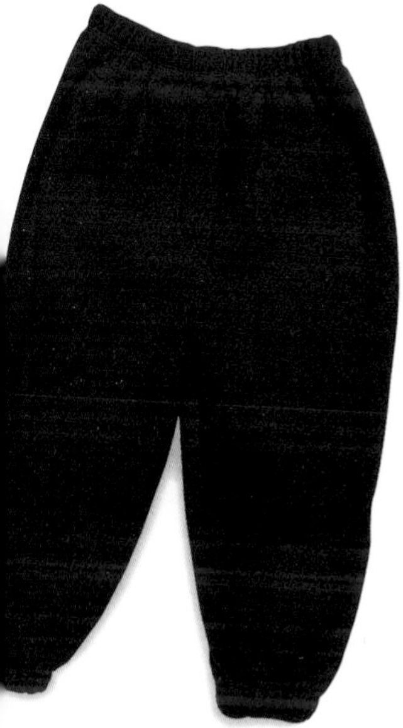

warm
trousers

cotton shorts

flowery
skirt

blue pants

Keeping warm

In cold weather, thick clothes keep us warm.

padded jacket

long scarf

warm hat

thick socks

I don’t feel cold in my big boots and cosy jacket.

woolly gloves

Keeping dry

Waterproof clothes keep us dry in wet weather.

wellington boots

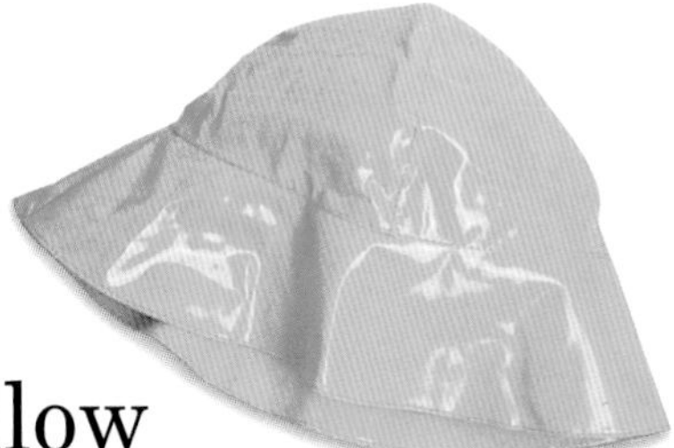

yellow rainhat

spotty umbrella

shiny raincoat

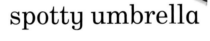

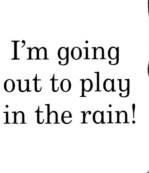

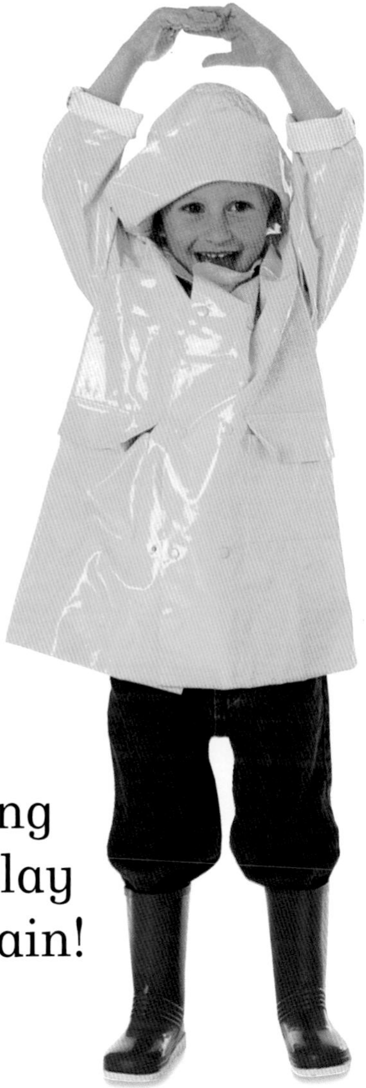

I'm going out to play in the rain!

Keeping cool

Thin, loose clothes
keep us cool
in hot weather.

summe
shirt

plastic sandals

baseball c

straw sunhat

I wear a
T-shirt when
it is sunny.

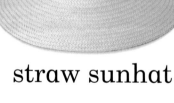

red sundress

Night clothes

Ve put on cosy,
omfortable clothes
t bedtime.

baby
sleepsuit

d nightdress

dressing gown

rabbit slippers

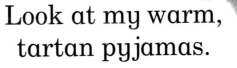

Look at my warm,
tartan pyjamas.

Sporty clothes

There are many different kinds of sporty clothes.

training shoes

hooded sweatshi

stretchy leggings

swimming costume

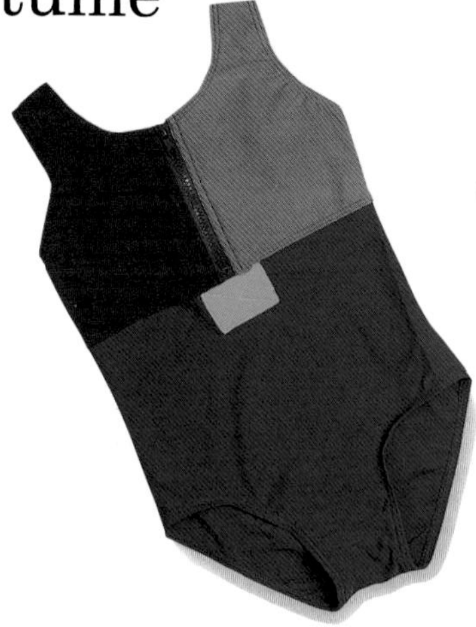

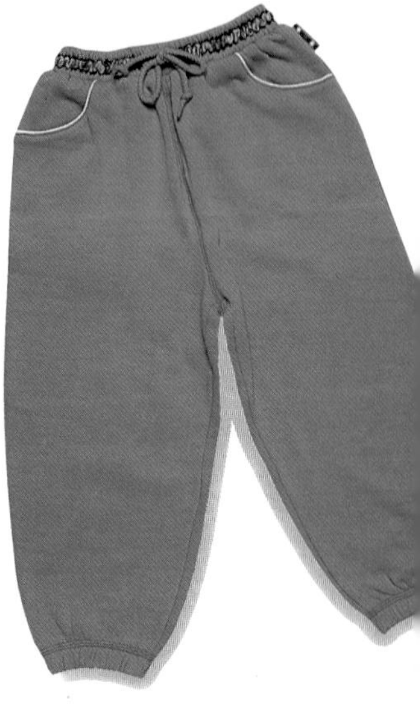

jogging pants

Have you ever been roller skating?

shiny
leotard

ski
fleece

swimming
trunks

games
shirt

plimsolls

I wear
special
boots to
play
football.

Baby clothes

Baby clothes are small and soft.

yellow vest

red vest

cotton shoes

fleecy bonnet

Why do you think this suit has poppers?

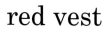

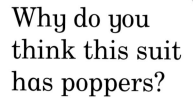

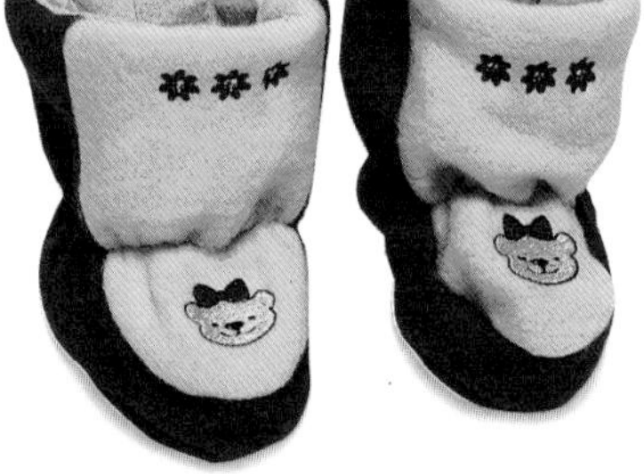

pram shoes

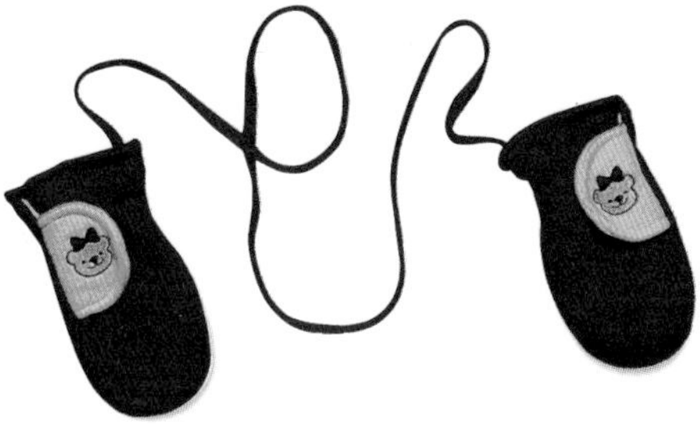

tiny
mittens

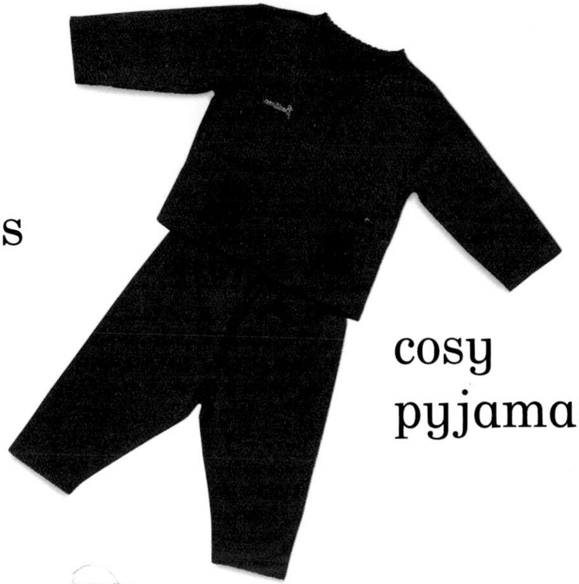

cosy
pyjamas

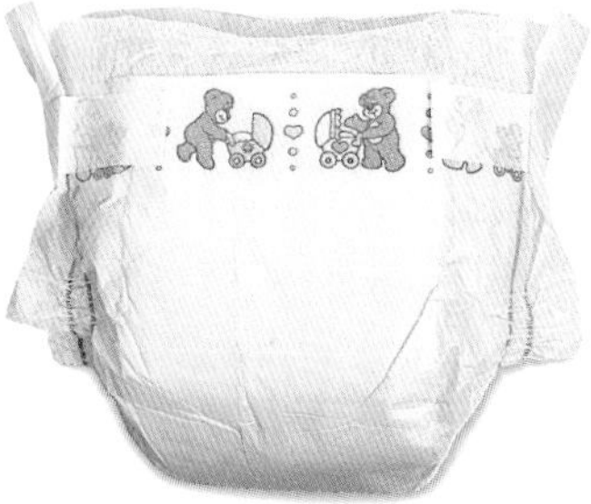

padded nappy

towelling bib

nug snowsuit

Which clothes
would baby
wear on a
cold day?

Patterned clothes

Sometimes, clothes are brightly patterned.

checked trousers

tartan braces

stripey T-shirt

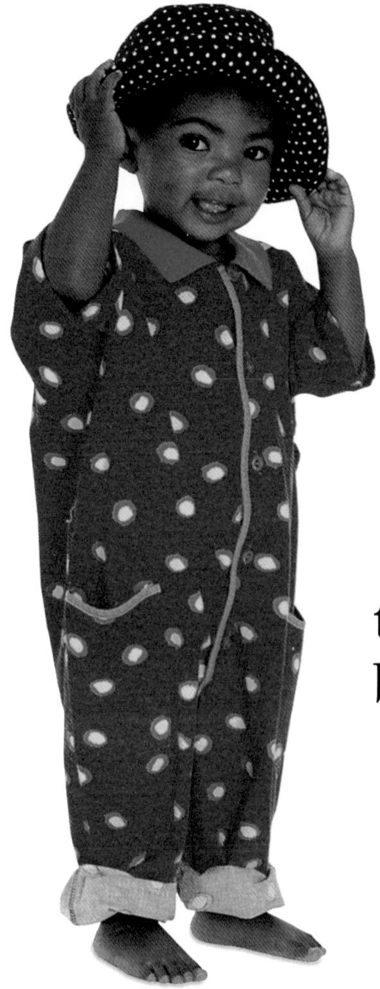

I like spotty clothes!

checked socks

checked shirt

stripey tights

stripey trousers

tartan skirt

I'm covered in flowers!

Fancy dress clothes

Do you like dressing up in disguises?

pirate's eye patch

cowboy hat

silver mask

clown's nose

clown's hat

I'm a little flower.

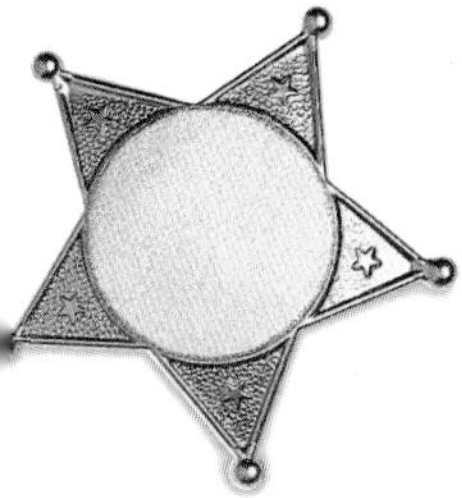

sheriff's
badge

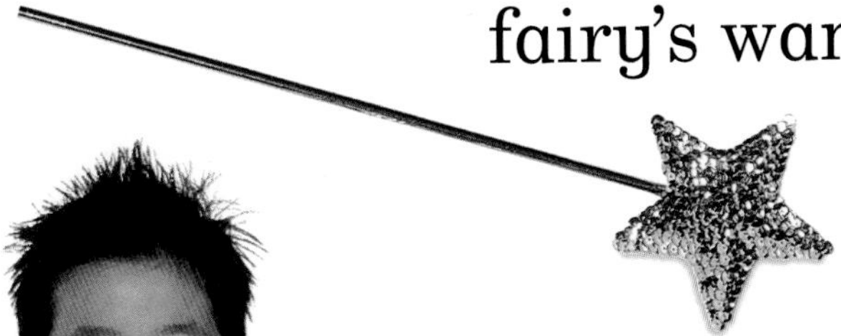

fairy's wand

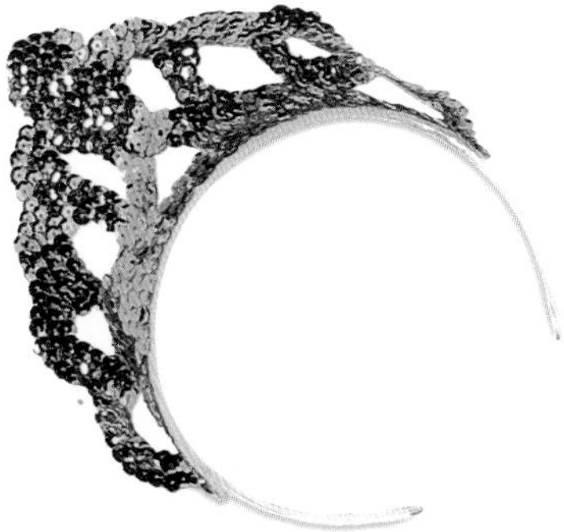

princess's
tiara

wizard's hat

pirate's
hat

What am I dressed up as? Grrrr!

Bits and pieces

Sometimes, we wear different things with our clothes.

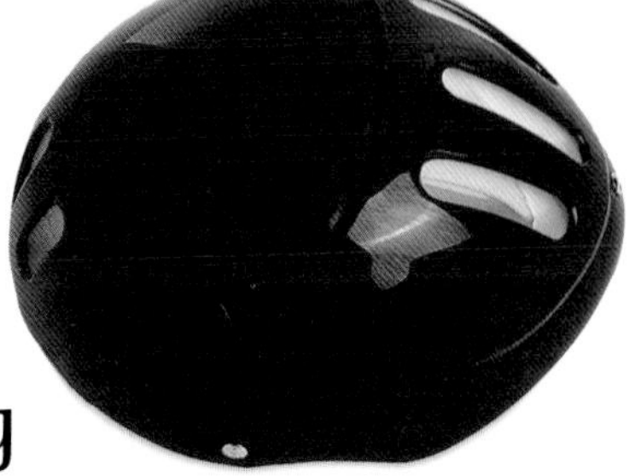

safety helmet

blue tie

elastic belt

Why do you think this is called an overall?

catcher's mitt

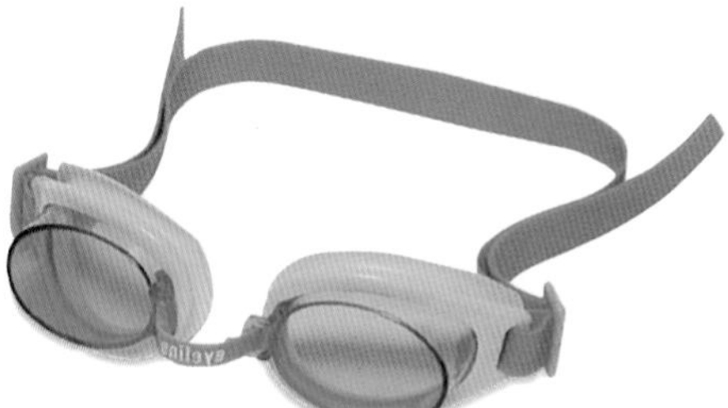

swimming goggles

wrist watch

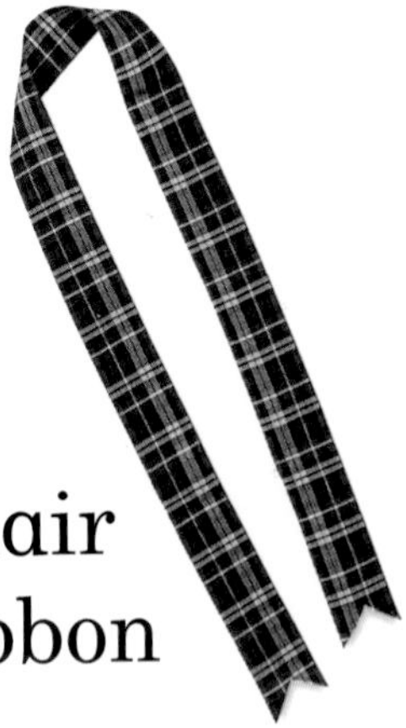

hair ribbon

cooking apron

snazzy sunglasses

bow tie

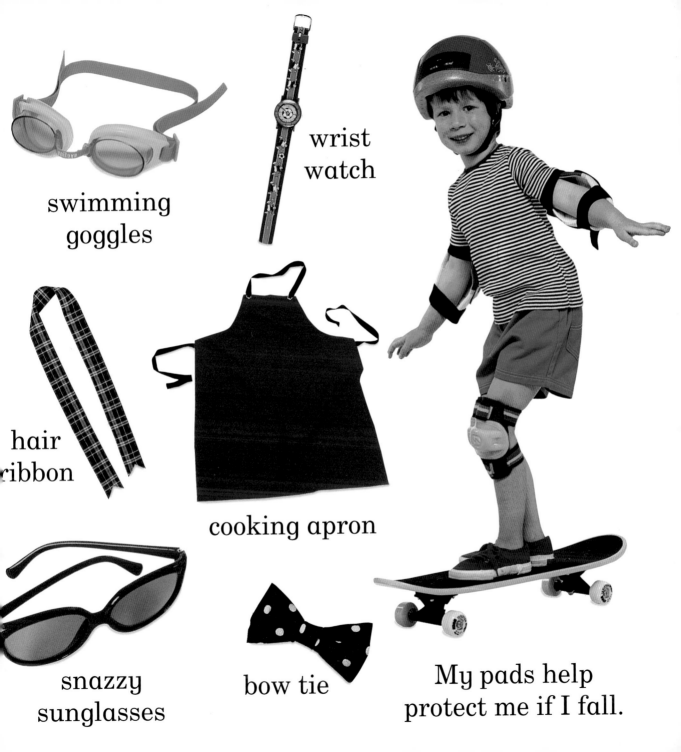

My pads help protect me if I fall.

Can you remember the names of all these different clothes?